A Cashless Society

Nicolas Brasch

NELSON
CENGAGE Learning

Australia • Brazil • Japan • Korea • Mexico • Singapore • Spain • United Kingdom • United States

A Cashless Society

Fast Forward
Silver Level 23

Text: Nicolas Brasch
Editor: Cameron Macintosh
Design: Ami Sharpe
Series design: James Lowe
Production controller: Seona Galbally
Photo research: Fiona Smith
Audio recordings: Juliet Hill, Picture Start
Spoken by: Matthew King and Abbe Holmes

Acknowledgements
The author and publisher would like to acknowledge permission to reproduce material from the following sources: Photographs by AAP Image/Dave Hunt, p 22; Alamy/Joe Wardman, p 12/ Llene MacDonald, p 14; Corbis/Christine Kolisch, p 4/ James Leynse, pp 18, 19/ Polak Matt/Corbis Sygma, p 9; Gettyimages/David Young-Wolff, p 5/ Ken Reid, back cover, p 10/ Michael Matisse, p 17; iStockphoto/Kay Ransom, p 23/ Sami Suni, p 11 bottom/ Sean Locke, p 6; Newspix/Brett Costello, p 7; PhotoEdit/Michael Newman, p 8/ Photolibrary/Corbis Corporation, p 15/ Steve Horrell, p 16/ Workbook, Inc/Matsui Tim, cover, p 13.

ISBN 978 0 17 012698 4
ISBN 978 0 17 012693 9 (set)

Cengage Learning Australia
Level 7, 80 Dorcas Street
South Melbourne, Victoria Australia 3205
Phone: 1300 790 853

Cengage Learning New Zealand
Unit 4B Rosedale Office Park
331 Rosedale Road, Albany, North Shore NZ 0632
Phone: 0800 449 725

For learning solutions, visit **cengage.com.au**

Printed in Australia by Ligare Pty Ltd
5 6 7 8 9 10 11 20 19 18 17 16

THE UNIVERSITY OF MELBOURNE

Evaluated in independent research by staff from the Department of Language, Literacy and Arts Education at the University of Melbourne.

A Cashless Society

Nicolas Brasch

Contents

Chapter 1

A SHORT HISTORY OF MONEY

For thousands of years, people have traded by swapping precious objects for goods and services. Many different objects have been used for these **transactions.**

People have used shells, feathers and even tea bricks, which are small bricks made by pressing wet tea leaves together.

tea bricks have been used for money in parts of Asia

Eventually, most societies around the world created coins and notes to use as money.
Coins and notes were easier for people to carry around than the other objects they had used.

Today, thanks to technology and innovative thinking, there are many ways to carry out a financial transaction without the need to use **cash**.
This has led to the term "cashless society".

Chapter 2

CHEQUES

A cheque is a piece of paper that **authorises** the transfer of money from one person to another. Cheques are issued by banks to their customers.

When customers want to use a cheque
to make a transaction,
they have to write four things onto the cheque:

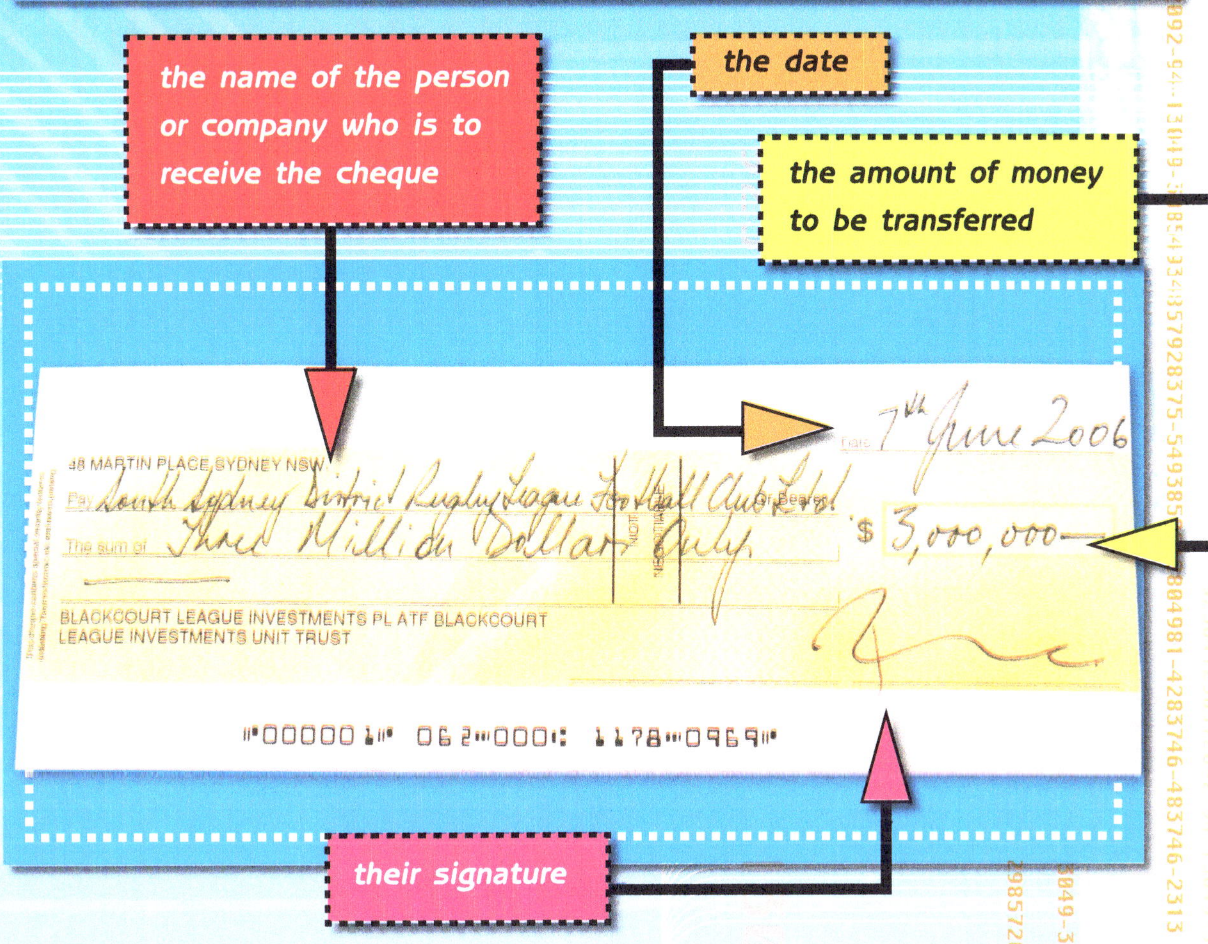

A bank will only allow the transfer of funds to take place
when the signature has been checked
against an original signature held by the bank.

Advantages of Cheques

The main advantage of using a cheque is that it enables large amounts of money to be transferred without the need to physically exchange a large amount of cash. This makes the transaction safer.

Disadvantages of Cheques

The main disadvantage of using a cheque is that cheques are subject to forgery. Forgery means that a person pretends to be another person and uses the other person's cheques to pay for things. However, banks have a policy of waiting at least three days before finalising a cheque transaction. This gives people who know they have had cheques stolen time to cancel a **forged** transaction.

Chapter 3

CARDS

During the 20th century, different types of cards that carried out the functions of money came into existence.

The four main types of cards are:

- credit cards
- debit cards
- prepayment cards
- smart cards.

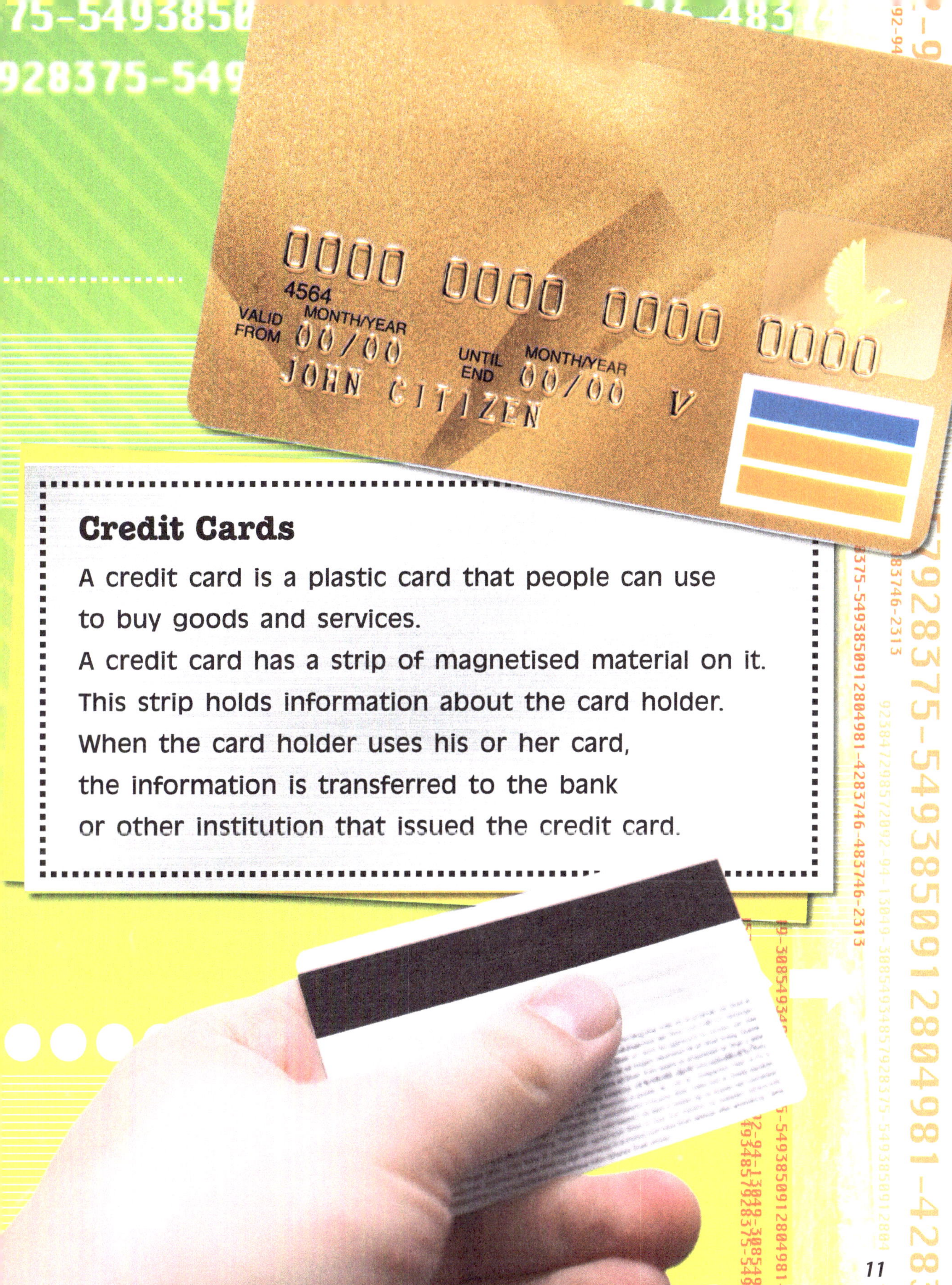

Credit Cards

A credit card is a plastic card that people can use to buy goods and services.

A credit card has a strip of magnetised material on it. This strip holds information about the card holder. When the card holder uses his or her card, the information is transferred to the bank or other institution that issued the credit card.

Unlike cheques, which require the amount of money being transferred to be in the cheque holder's bank account, credit cards allow people to spend money that they haven't yet earned. They are then sent a monthly bill that outlines how much they have to pay back that month.

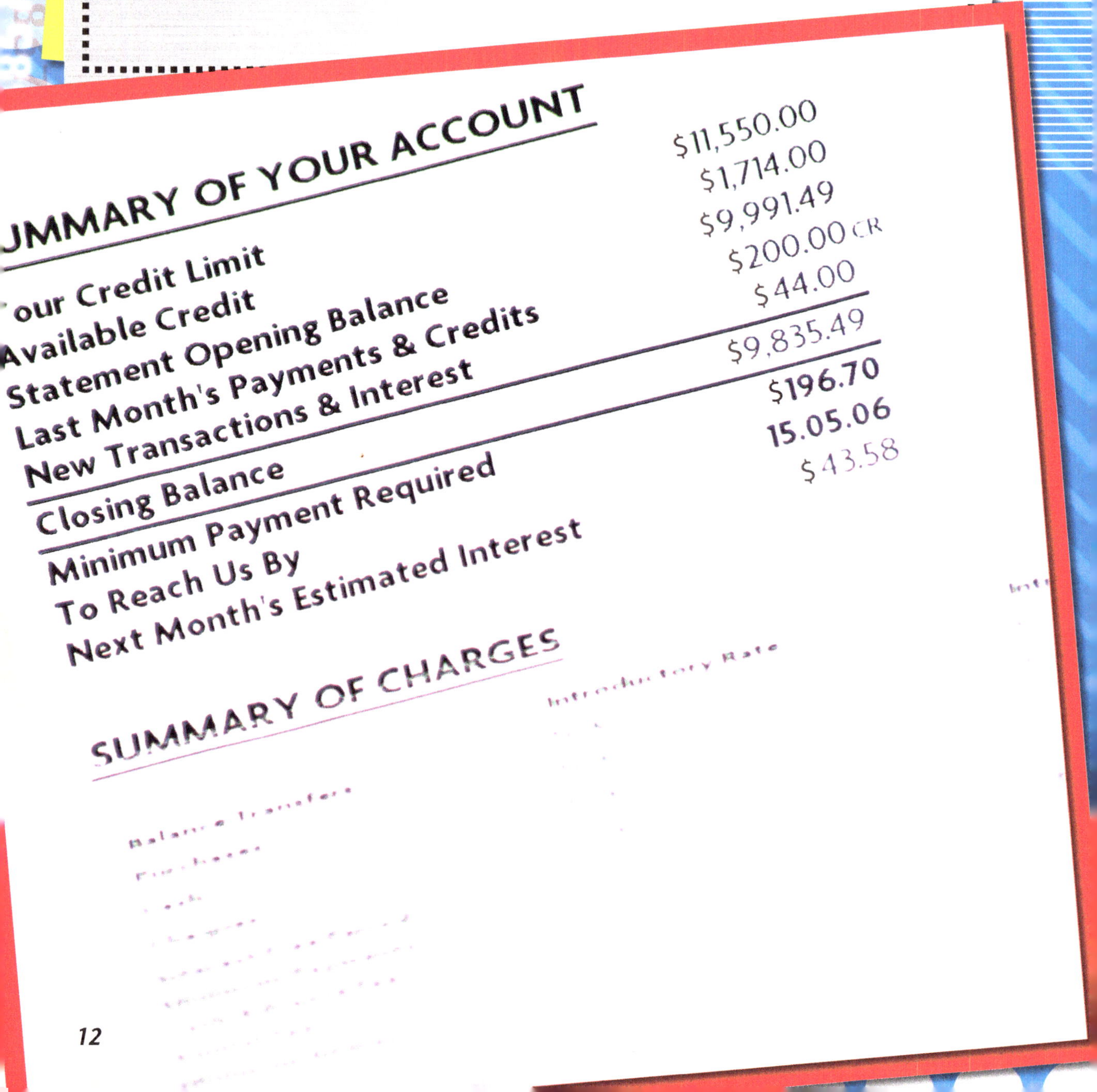

UMMARY OF YOUR ACCOUNT

our Credit Limit	$11,550.00
Available Credit	$1,714.00
Statement Opening Balance	$9,991.49
Last Month's Payments & Credits	$200.00 CR
New Transactions & Interest	$44.00
Closing Balance	$9,835.49
Minimum Payment Required	$196.70
To Reach Us By	15.05.06
Next Month's Estimated Interest	$43.58

SUMMARY OF CHARGES

Advantages of Credit Cards

Credit cards are easy to carry around.
They also enable people to buy goods and services in an emergency if they don't have the money to pay for them.

Disadvantages of Credit Cards

The main disadvantage of credit cards is that people can get into financial trouble by spending more money than they can afford to pay back.

Debit Cards

A debit card is a plastic card similar to a credit card. The major difference between debit cards and credit cards is that a debit card only allows a person to spend money that is in his or her bank account.

This helps overcome the main disadvantage of credit cards.

So, people who use a debit card cannot get into the same level of financial trouble as someone using a credit card. The bank issuing the debit card won't allow a transaction to go through if the card holder doesn't have enough money in his or her bank account.

Prepayment Cards

Prepayment cards are usually made from plastic or cardboard.
They are cards that have a certain amount of money stored in them.
The money is stored as information in a magnetised strip or a microchip.
A person buys the card for the same amount of money that is stored in the card.
He or she then uses the card until the amount of money stored in the card has run out.

The most common use of prepayment cards is for telecommunications.
People can insert their card into a public phone and make telephone calls without the need to put in cash.
Prepayment cards are very popular in Japan.

Smart Cards

Smart cards look similar to credit cards. They are usually used for small transactions, and replace the need for people to carry cash around with them.

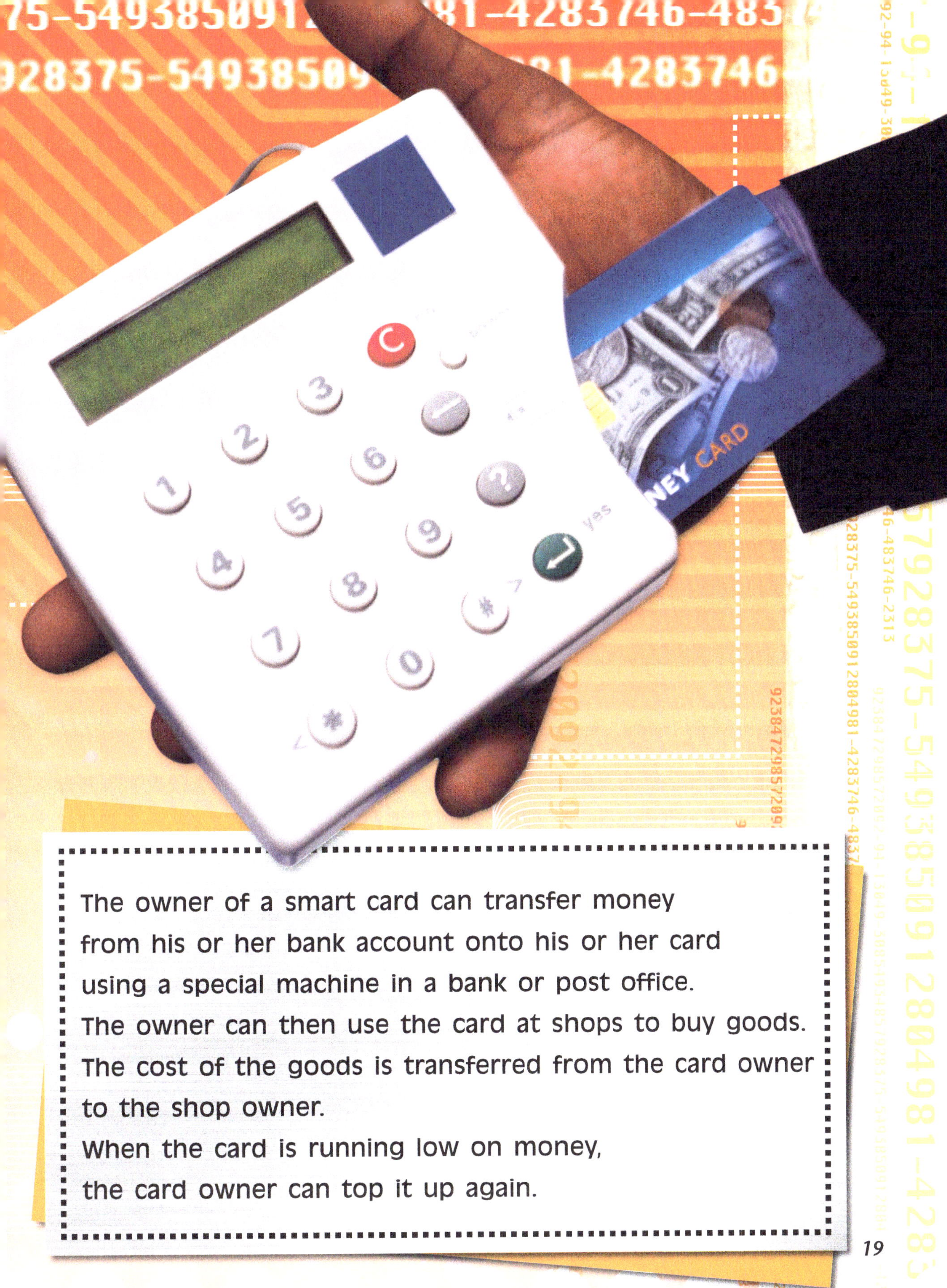

The owner of a smart card can transfer money from his or her bank account onto his or her card using a special machine in a bank or post office.
The owner can then use the card at shops to buy goods.
The cost of the goods is transferred from the card owner to the shop owner.
When the card is running low on money, the card owner can top it up again.

Chapter 4

ELECTRONIC BANKING

Electronic banking involves the transfer of funds through messages sent electronically between two or more banks or other types of financial institutions. Two of the most common types of electronic banking are direct deposits and direct debits. Direct deposits are amounts of money paid into a person's bank account from another account. This is now a very common way for companies to pay the wages of their workforce.

Jenny Customer
54 Somewhere Ave
Savingsville 3672

a direct deposit

Super Saver Account Transaction Details

Date	Transaction	Debit	Credit	Balance
01 Apr	2007 OPENING BALANCE			$2,560.50
01 Apr	ATM	50.00		$2.510.50
04 Apr	FUNCORP		2,400.25	$4,910.75
05 Apr	CHEQUE 3422	110.00		
05 Apr	ATM	60.00		$4740.75
08 Apr	CHEQUE 3423	56.00		$4684.75
11 Apr	ATM	80.00		$4604.75

Jenny Customer
54 Somewhere Ave
Savingsville 3672

Super Saver Account Transaction Details

direct debits

Date	Transaction	Debit	Credit	Balance
01 May	**2007 OPENING BALANCE**			**$3,500.40**
02 May	CHEQUE	60.00		$3,440.40
05 May	FUNCORP		2,400.25	$5,840.65
08 May	CHEQUE 3427	100.00		$5,740.65
11 May	SPARK ELECTRICITY	55.00		$5,685.65
12 May	ATM	60.00		$5,625.65
14 May	DIAL-UP TELECOM	39.00		$5,586.65

Direct debit involves the holder of a bank account authorising a company to transfer regular amounts of money out of his or her bank account and into the company's bank account. People use direct debit to pay regular bills, such as telephone or electricity bills.

Chapter 5

INTERNET BANKING

The creation of the Internet has changed people's lives in many ways.
One major change is in the way people manage their bank accounts.
Internet banking allows people to view their accounts, pay bills and transfer money at home using their personal computers, all without having to go into a bank.

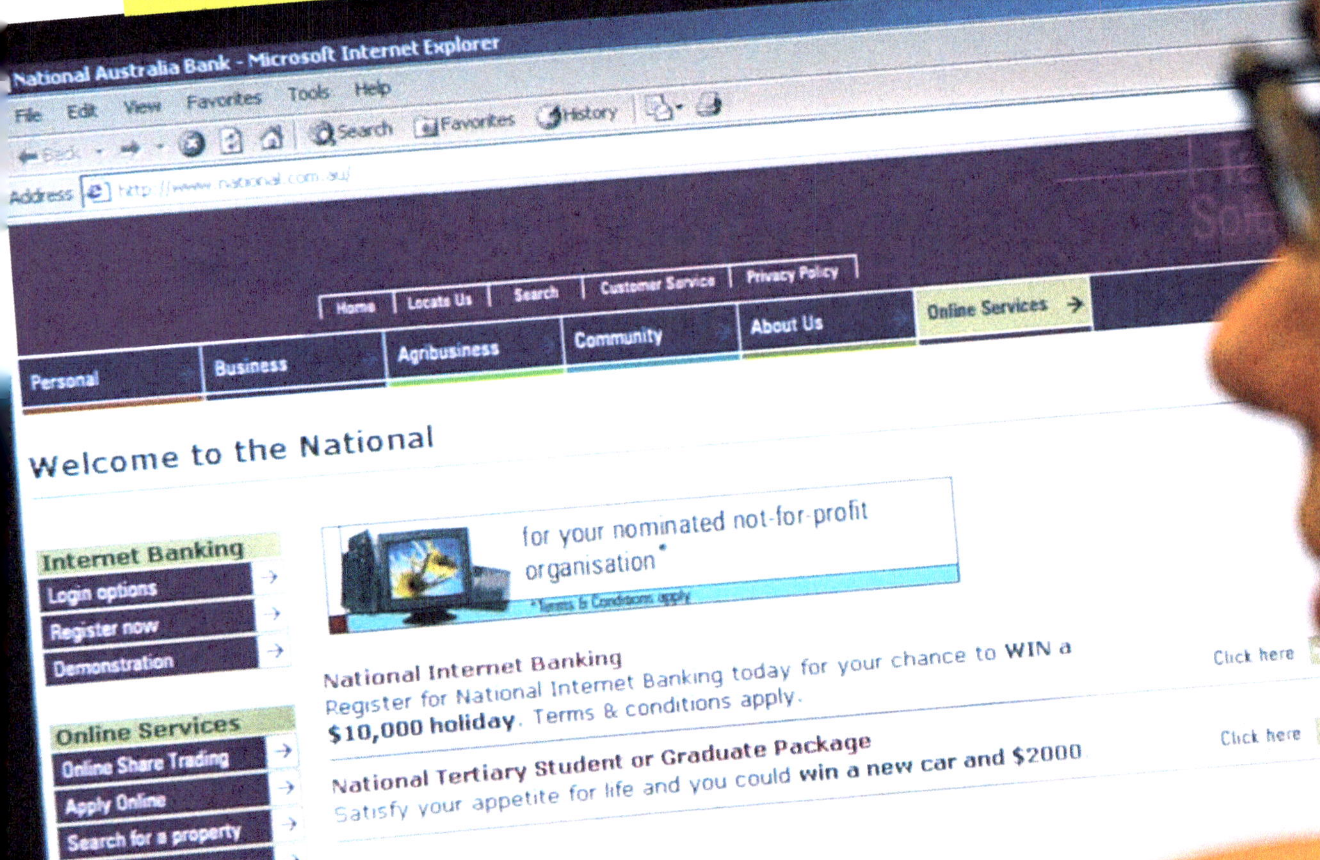

Banks put major security procedures in place to stop anyone but the real account holder from accessing their bank account over the Internet. This helps to ensure that people's bank accounts are safe.

Glossary

authorises gives permission to do something

cash money in the form of notes and coins

forged copied illegally

transactions exchanges or transfers of goods or money

Index